The Black Geese

A Baba Yaga Story from Russia

Retold by Alison Lurie • Illustrated by Jessica Souhami

A DK INK BOOK
DK PUBLISHING, INC.

Long ago there lived a man and wife who had two
children, a girl and a boy. One day the woman said
to her daughter, "Elena, we are going to market today.
Stay in the house while we are away, and look after
your baby brother, for Baba Yaga's black geese who
steal children have been seen flying over the village.
When we come home, we will bring you some
sugar buns."

After her mother and father were gone, Elena stayed
in the house with her brother for a little while.
But soon she got tired of this and took him outside
to where her friends were playing. She put him down
on the grass and joined in their games, and presently
she forgot all about him.

The black geese came down, seized the little boy, and carried him away.

When Elena found her brother gone, she was very frightened. She shouted his name, but he did not answer. At last she said to herself that the black geese must have stolen her brother and taken him to Baba Yaga, the terrible witch of the forest, who is eight feet tall and eats little children.

"I must go after him," Elena said. And she began to run toward the forest.

She ran across the fields and came to a pond, and there she saw a fish lying on the bank, gasping for water.

"Elena, Elena!" it called. "I am dying!"

Elena wanted to hurry on, but she was sorry for the fish. So she picked it up and put it carefully in the pond, where it sank and then rose again to the surface.

"As you have helped me, so I shall help you," said the fish. "Here, take this shell. If ever you are in danger, throw it over your shoulder."

Elena did not see how a shell could help her, but she did not want to seem rude, so she put it in her pocket and ran on.

Presently she came to a grove of trees, and there she saw a squirrel caught in a trap.

"Elena, Elena!" it called. "My leg is caught!" Elena wanted to go on, but she felt sorry for the squirrel. So she released the trap. The squirrel darted up into a tree and down again.

"As you have helped me, so I shall help you," it said. "Here, take this walnut. If ever you are in danger, throw it over your shoulder."

Elena put the nut in her pocket and hurried on.

Soon she came to a stony bank, and there she saw a field mouse trying to move a fallen rock.

"Elena, Elena!" it called. "I cannot get into my hole!" Elena was sorry for the field mouse, so she pushed and shoved until she had moved the rock aside. The mouse darted into its hole and reappeared.

"As you have helped me, so I shall help you," it said. "Take this pebble. If ever you are in danger, throw it over your shoulder."

Elena put the pebble in her pocket and ran on into the dark forest.

The trees grew so close together that not a speck of
sunshine could get through. Soon Elena came to a clearing,
and there she saw Baba Yaga's hut, which stands on
three giant hens' legs and can move around when it likes.
The black geese were roosting on the roof of the hut.

Baba Yaga was asleep inside, snoring through her long nose. Near her on the floor sat Elena's little brother, playing with some bones.

Elena crept into the hut and picked up her brother. But as she ran away into the forest, the black geese saw her. They began to honk and to clap their wings, and Baba Yaga woke up.

"Stop, thief!" she screamed. "Bring back my dinner!"

Elena did not stop, or answer the witch, but hurried on with her little brother in her arms; and Baba Yaga came out of her hut and started after them on her long bony legs.

Elena could not run very fast, because her brother was too heavy. When she came out of the forest and looked back, she saw that the witch was gaining on them.

What could she do?

Suddenly she remembered what the fish had said, so she reached
into her pocket and threw the shell over her shoulder.

At once a broad lake appeared behind her. It was too large for
Baba Yaga to go around it, so she squatted down by the edge and
began to drink. She drank so fast that the water began to sink at
once, and it was not long before she had drunk up the whole lake.
Then she ran on.

Elena looked back and saw that the lake was gone and that Baba Yaga was gaining on them again. She remembered what the squirrel had said, reached into her pocket, and threw the walnut over her shoulder.

At once a thick grove of trees sprang up behind her. They grew so close together that Baba Yaga could not get through. So she began to chew up the trees with her sharp teeth. She ate so fast that in a few minutes she had eaten up the whole grove of trees. Then she ran on.

Elena looked back again and saw that the trees were gone
and the witch was coming after her again, so close that she
could hear her gnashing her long teeth and see her reaching out
her bony arms. Elena felt in her pocket and threw the pebble
over her shoulder.

Instantly a stony mountain sprang up behind her, so tall that
its top was lost in clouds. Baba Yaga could not eat it or drink it;
and she could not get over it. So she had to go back into the forest,
growling and cursing.

As for Elena, she went on to her village and was
safe at home playing with her little brother when her
father and mother got back from the market with the
sugar buns.

Alison Lurie's *The Black Geese* can be found in her collection
Clever Gretchen and Other Forgotten Folktales.
The story is based partly on "The Magic Swan-Geese" from *Russian Fairy Tales*
by Aleksandr Afanasyev, published by Random House.

DK PUBLISHING, INC.
95 Madison Avenue
New York, NY 10016
Visit us on the World Wide Web at http://www.dk.com

Library of Congress Cataloging-in-Publication Data
Lurie, Alison.
    The black geese / by Alison Lurie : illustrated by Jessica Souhami. — 1st ed.
        p.   cm.
    "A DK Ink book."
    Summary: When her little brother is taken away by the black geese belonging
to the terrible witch Baba Yaga, Elena searches for him in the great dark forest.
    ISBN 0–7894–2558–0
    1. Baba Yaga (Legendary character)—Legends. [1. Baba Yaga (Legendary character)—Legends.
2. Fairy tales. 3. Folklore—Russia.] I. Souhami, Jessica, ill. II. Title.
PZ8.1.L974Bl 1998   98–3681
398.2'094701—dc21   CIP
                                                                               AC

Book design by Jessica Souhami and Paul McAlinden
The illustrations for this book are watercolor-painted paper, cut and collaged, and pen and ink.
The text of this book is set in 18 point Monotype Bodoni.

Printed and bound in Hong Kong

First American Edition, 1999
2 4 6 8 10 9 7 5 3 1

Published simultaneously in Great Britain by Frances Lincoln Limited,
4 Torriano Mews, London NW5 2RZ